Farm

Yummy Scrummy!

Ashley Birch

EGMONT

This book belongs to:

....

With special thanks to Valerie Wilding
For Lauren and Jake

EGMONT

We bring stories to life

Magic Farm: Yummy Scrummy!
First published in Great Britain 2011
by Egmont UK Limited
239 Kensington High Street
London W8 6SA

ISBN 978 1 4052 5528 8

1 3 5 7 9 10 8 6 4 2

www.egmont.co.uk

A CIP catalogue record for this title is available from the British Library

Printed and bound in Great Britain by the CPI Group

CONTENTS

Raspberry Ripples

Olly hopped from one foot to the other. 'Can we taste it yet?'

'No!' His sister, Hannah, laughed. 'You can't have raspberry ripple ice-cream without the raspberry ripple, can you? You'll have to wait!'

Olly passed her a bowl of deep pink purée. 'Made from our own Golden Valley Farm raspberries!' he said. The Thompson family were proud of their farm. They hadn't lived there long, but already they had lots of animals, some home-grown fruit and vegetables, and a small herb garden.

They were learning things every day.

Hannah stirred raspberry purée into the ice-cream mixture. It had already been partly frozen, and icy

glints twinkled here and there as she blended the deep pink swirls. 'Doesn't that look gorgeous?' she said. 'We can sell it at the farmers' market – as long as you don't eat it all, Olly!' She scooped up a large spoonful for Olly to taste.

'It's smooth,' he said. 'And lovely and creamy. But . . .'

Hannah tried it too. 'Hmmm. Something's not quite right, is it?'

'More sugar?' wondered Olly.

'More cream?' suggested Hannah.

'Let's have another taste!' said Olly.

They each took another spoonful. 'More ripple!' they said at exactly the same time.

'We need to go and pick some more

raspberries,' said Hannah. She put

the ice-cream mixture in the fridge.

Olly grabbed two baskets. Together

they ran out to the field where the

raspberries grew. Max, their black

and white sheepdog, barked loudly,

as if to say, 'I'm coming, too!'

The raspberries hung like little

bundles of pink bells on the fresh green

leaves. Olly couldn't resist popping one or two into his mouth as he filled his basket. He would never eat berries if he didn't know what they were – but he knew these were safe to eat.

But then something caught Olly's eye. Max was racing across the field towards the paddock, where Olly could see Golden Valley Farm's newest addition. A tiny little foal! She was only a few days old. She had enormous dark eyes fringed by long lashes, and her conker-coloured coat was soft and glossy. The foal was

reaching through the fence to sniff some plants. Her mother, Ebony, was nearby watching.

'Heel, Max!' Olly cried as they ran after him.

Too late. Max had already reached the fence. But instead of barking, he sat down and craned his head upwards. The foal stretched down, and their noses touched. Max's tail wagged madly, and the foal made high-pitched whinnying sounds.

'Sweet!' said Hannah. She stroked the foal's nose. 'I wish we could think

of the right name for you.'

Olly, Hannah and their parents had spent hours trying to decide on a name. Sammy? Silky? Lulu? No. They just couldn't agree.

Max was still trying to rub noses with the foal, but she was more interested in some plants with long green leaves, growing by the fence.

She could just about reach them and started nibbling away happily.

'What *is* that plant?' asked Olly, a puzzled look on his face.

'I don't know,' said Hannah, 'but she's enjoying it!' She peered into Olly's basket. 'Come on, we've got enough raspberries between us.'

Olly followed her slowly, deep

in thought. But Hannah was getting impatient.

'Come on, slow coach! You're thinking about the plant, aren't you?' she said. 'You always *have* to know what everything is. Well, I'm going to make the ice-cream. Come, Max!'

Olly followed his sister, promising himself he'd pop back later and have another good look at those leaves.

'I'll be a plant expert one day,' he called ahead to her. 'You just watch!'

Back in the kitchen, Hannah and Olly sieved the berries and added sugar. Just as they were swirling all the extra purée into their mixture, there was a sharp bang at the door.

A voice called, 'Farm inspector here! Annual inspection time. Line your sheep up in twos immediately.'

Olly's mouth fell open.

'We'd better find Mum and Dad,' whispered Hannah.

The door opened and a long leg appeared. In came their best friend, Aidan Longman!

Olly laughed – he was so relieved it wasn't a farm inspector. He should have guessed it was Aidan. Line up the sheep indeed!

'Ooh, what's that?' Aidan asked when he saw the pink and cream swirly mixture. He went to stick a finger in it.

'Don't!' Hannah cried. 'We can't sell

ice-cream with germs! Get a spoon.'

Aidan fetched something from the drawer, and Olly grinned when he saw what it was.

'Hannah,' said Aidan, 'can I have a spoonful of ice-cream now, please?'

'Go on,' she replied.

From behind his back, Aidan whipped out a huge ladle!

Hannah couldn't help laughing. 'I meant a teaspoon!' She fetched three small spoons and they all tasted the mixture.

'Excellent,' said Olly.

'Perfect!' cried Hannah.

'It's not very cold,' said Aidan.

'It's not been frozen yet,' explained Olly. 'You'll have to wait a couple of hours.'

Aidan's eyes sparkled. 'Hey, I know! Why don't we have some fun till the ice-cream's ready for us?

Let's go to Magic Farm.'

Olly and Hannah's hands met in a high-five. 'Yes!'

Poor Muck

Olly put the ice-cream mixture into the freezer, and the three friends raced outside and headed uphill.

'I wonder what the Hayseeds are up to,' said Olly.

'Something magical, I bet,' said Hannah.

The Hayseeds – Patch, Tishoo, Sunny and Muck – ran Magic Farm. They weren't ordinary farmers. They were walking, talking scarecrows! They had woken up on the farm one morning and found that the farmer was missing. They were looking after things until he came back. *If* he came back! The Hayseeds were good at farming, but didn't always get it quite right. Olly, Hannah and Aidan had already helped them out of some sticky situations . . .

The friends reached the hilltop and started down the other side, going faster and faster. Halfway down was a scarecrow with an arm outstretched.

Below it, mist swirled in the valley.

As always, Aidan reached the scarecrow first.

He grabbed hold of its arm and span it round, running in a wide circle alongside it. Then he disappeared! One moment Aidan was there, and the next – he was gone!

Olly blinked, then grinned. This was the scarecrow's secret, and it amazed Olly every time.

'My turn,' said Hannah. She took

hold of the scarecrow's arm and swung round with her hair flying out behind her. She vanished as quickly as Aidan had.

Now it was Olly's turn. He grasped the outstretched arm, feeling the prickle of straw poking through the thin sleeve. Round he went, spinning the scarecrow.

Whooosh! He was swept into a silvery whirlwind.

Olly let go of the scarecrow's arm, and stumbled forward. 'Ooof!'

'Watch out!' said Aidan, as Olly crashed into him and they toppled over. 'Sorry, Olly, I forgot to get out of the way. I was looking at the sky!' Little puffy clouds, tinted pale gold,

pink and blue bobbed in the breeze,

high above them. The sun glittered

like a giant diamond, sending out

rainbow-coloured sparks.

The three friends walked towards the farm. A creeper rambled over the pretty farmhouse, glowing scarlet in the sunlight. Olly noticed that the front door stood open, and the fields and farmyard were deserted.

'There's not a Hayseed in sight,' Olly muttered.

'And I can't see any Little Rotters,'

said Hannah, looking all around.

The Little Rotters were naughty creatures who loved causing trouble for the poor scarecrows. They were always messing things up on Magic Farm, and the Hayseeds were afraid of them. A Little Rotter could sneak up and pull out a scarecrow's stuffing in no time!

'We'd better see if everything's all right,' Olly said.

Aidan, with his long legs, jumped the white picket fence, while the others climbed over. 'Hey!' he said, craning his neck. 'Something's going on in the orchard!'

'Heee-ee-lp!' shrieked a voice.

Olly climbed a log pile for a better

view but, before he reached the top, a scruffy scarecrow, splodged with mud, tore past. He was chased by two grinning creatures with tufts of orange hair. Little Rotters!

'Catching you!' yelled one.

'Muck!' Olly called to the scarecrow. 'We're here!'

'We'll help you,' cried Hannah.

'We're not scared of Little Rotters!'

Muck ran in circles, waving his arms wildly.

Olly chased after him, but Aidan

overtook and put his hands firmly on the scarecrow's shoulders. 'Get behind me, Muck,' he said. 'I'll protect you.' He faced the Little Rotters, with Muck cowering behind him.

'Watch out, Aidan!' Olly yelled. 'They're going to throw something at you!'

The Little Rotters were clutching

strange, spotty green and purple balls, the size of grapefruits. They squealed with laughter and aimed.

Aidan shielded his face with his arms as the Little Rotters hurled the objects. One caught him right in the middle of his chest.

SPLAT!

To Olly's surprise, bright purple

mush exploded over Aidan's T-shirt.
That was no ball, he thought as the
Little Rotters ran off, screeching
with joy.

Olly and Hannah hurried over
to Aidan. Muck crouched behind
him, trembling.

'Are you OK, Aidan?' Olly asked.
'What was that?'

Hannah sniffed Aidan's T-shirt. 'It smells nice,' she said.

Aidan's face was red as he stared down at his stained front. He seemed to be struggling to speak. 'Phhh . . . bla . . . gor . . . Those . . . little . . . little . . .'

'Rotters?' Hannah suggested.

Hayseeds in Hiding

'Those Little Rotters better watch out!' Aidan exclaimed.

'They've gone,' said Olly. He peered at Aidan's messy top, then reached out a finger and scooped off a dollop of the sticky purple mush.

'Don't you dare eat that, Olly!' Hannah grabbed his hand to stop him sticking his finger in his mouth. 'You don't know what it is.'

Muck peered round Aidan's left knee. 'It's OK, Olly,' he said, his voice shaking. 'It's fruit from our orchard, so it's safe. You can eat anything that grows on Magic Farm!'

Olly touched the tip of his tongue to his finger and tasted. Mmmm! The fruit was delicious – sweet and slightly tangy. 'Try it!' he said.

Aidan scraped off a blob from his T-shirt. A big grin lit up his face. 'Scrummy!'

Hannah picked up a whole fruit

that had missed Aidan. Breaking it open, she held it out. 'What is it?'

'Dunno,' said Olly. 'What's it called, Muck?'

'We don't know,' Muck answered. He was still trembling. 'Last week we went to the orchard and we found these growing. A few on each bush. But now there are hundreds and hundreds. We need to harvest it all or it will rot. Then it will go to waste and cause a terrible mess. Oh my, yes.'

Hannah licked her lips. 'I think you should call this fruit the gurple, because it's part green, part purple.'

'Good name!' Olly licked his juice-stained hands.

'Let's go to the orchard before

the Little Rotters come back,' Muck said. 'There's so much ripe fruit and it keeps falling off the trees. We're having trouble keeping up with it.'

'OK,' said Olly. There was always something delicious to eat at the orchard. Magic Farm fruit grew just when and where it wanted to – magic! 'It sounds as if you need some help.

In fact, I know the answer to your problem!'

Muck stopped. 'You do?'

Olly spread his hands. 'The Duzzit, of course!' The Duzzit was the scarecrows' special farm machine. It had handles and buttons and arms for all sorts of different jobs.

'What a good idea!' Muck clapped

Olly on the back. 'Let's go!'

As Olly led the way to the orchard, he heard a yell behind him. Hannah was on her knees examining her sticky, purple hands.

'I slipped on a squashed gurple,' she said. 'I'm filthy. Look at me!'

'Look at the *ground*,' said Aidan.

Olly couldn't believe his eyes.

There was squashed fruit all over the place, and they hadn't even reached the trees yet. And what were those squealing noises? Oh no . . .

'Little Rotters!' Hannah gasped.

Eight or nine of the naughty little creatures were running in and out of the orchard, throwing fruit at each other.

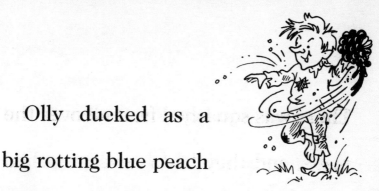

Olly ducked as a big rotting blue peach sailed towards him. 'Missed!' he shouted. He stood up again, and was splattered with giant blackberries. 'Oi! Stop!'

But the Little Rotters gathered armfuls of the squishy fruit lying beneath the trees, and kept on throwing it at the friends. Olly had to dart to one side to avoid a fat melon as it hurtled through the air. He glanced over his shoulder as the fruit smashed on the ground, scattering huge seeds.

'That could have really hurt me!' Olly cried.

On the far side of the orchard, he

spotted the Duzzit. A yellow hat was peeping out from behind the purple machine.

'That's Sunny's hat!' he said. 'The rest of the Hayseeds must be hiding behind the Duzzit. Come on.'

Hannah held him back. 'You don't mean we should go right *through* the orchard, do you? Past all those Little

Rotters? I don't fancy getting hit by a pineapple or a mango.'

Just then Sunny popped her head up. 'Hey, kids! We're over here. Please he-elp!'

'We have to go and help,' Olly said. 'Even if Patch is brave enough to drive the Duzzit, the scarecrows can't harvest if they're getting pelted with

fruit by the Little Rotters. We'll have

to risk it.'

Hannah looked at the fruit flying

across the orchard. 'You mean . . .'

Olly nodded. *'Run for it!'*

Fruit Fight

Olly, Hannah and Aidan dodged between the trees, pulling poor Muck behind them. Two Little Rotters bombarded them with walnuts and another threw fruit at their legs.

Aidan trod on a squashed red banana and nearly went flying but, one after another, they managed to dive behind the Duzzit, landing beside their other scarecrow friends.

Sunny's usually happy face was solemn, and stained bright purple. Olly tried very hard not to giggle. The Hayseeds were just as splattered with squashed fruit as they were!

Patch patted everyone's heads and said, 'Most brave!'

Tishoo just sneezed. 'Ha-ha-hat-tishoo!' His hat shot into the air, but before it came down it was knocked sideways by a flying stripy pear.

The Duzzit tooted its whistle. *Wheeeeup! Wheeeeup!*

'It's pleased to see you,' said Sunny. She hugged Muck. 'We were worried about you.'

'I was worried too,' said Muck. 'But the children saved me.'

Hannah was watching the Rotters. 'If we lure them away,' she said, 'the Duzzit can start harvesting fruit.'

'But how can we?' Sunny asked.

An apple went sailing past her head and there was a burst of laughter from the Little Rotters.

'Hannah, Aidan and I will get them to chase us,' said Olly, 'so you can get the Duzzit going. OK?'

With a loud *Wheeeeup-up-up!* an arm swung out of the Duzzit's side. It held three giant umbrellas!

Muck looked puzzled. 'It's not raining.'

'It is,' said Olly, as they put up the umbrellas. 'It's raining rotten fruit!'

The children stepped out from behind the Duzzit. *Splat! Splat! Splat!* Overripe gurples smashed on to the umbrellas they were holding.

'Let's go!' said Aidan, and led the

way across the orchard.

A cry went up from the Little
Rotters. 'Nasty 'brellas!' They scooped
up more fruit and aimed lower this
time. As Olly and Hannah chased
after Aidan, they held their
umbrellas out like shields.
'Can't get us!' Olly yelled.

'Call yourselves Little

Rotters?' cried Aidan, reaching down to the ground. 'This gurple's more rotten than you.' He threw one of the purple and green fruits. It caught a Little Rotter right on its forehead, and exploded into purple mush. Juice ran down the angry little face.

'You can't catch meeeeee!' yelled Hannah, running through a thick

forest of currant bushes.

'Have a lubbly abble!' shouted a
Little Rotter. Olly ducked as a hard
orange apple whizzed overhead.

The children ran from bush to

bush as the Little Rotters threw any fruit they could lay their bony hands on. Behind them, the Duzzit let out a *chug chug a chug!* as it got ready for work.

Olly scrambled up the trunk of a nearby tree. Aidan and Hannah followed. 'Fingers crossed, they'll come after us. We need to keep them well away from the Hayseeds!'

With a happy *Wheeeup!* the Duzzit rumbled between rows of raspberry and tomato trees. Sunny and Muck sat on top, picking fruit, which they tossed to Tishoo. He posted it down different chutes that led into the Duzzit. He saw the children in the tree and gave them a thumbs up.

Hannah waved.

'Uh-oh!' said Olly. 'One of the Little Rotters saw you wave. He's signalling to the others.'

Aidan groaned. 'They've realised the Hayseeds are harvesting. We need to do something quickly!'

The Little Rotters started making their way back to the Duzzit. Olly spotted one of them creeping round towards the Hayseeds. It had a spotty pear in one hand and a massive gurple in the other.

'Oi! You!' Olly yelled, and waved his umbrella. 'Come and get me!'

'Hey!' Aidan shouted, leaping out of the tree. 'Get *me*!'

The Little Rotter raced back to

them with a squeal of rage. 'Nasty, nasty childrens!'

Hannah jumped down too and darted between bushes, shouting, 'Can't hit me!'

Suddenly, the biggest Little Rotter shouted to the others. They began to gather as many gurples into their arms as possible. Then they charged straight at the Duzzit.

The Hayseeds shrieked in fright.

'Oh no!' said Aidan. 'They're pushing gurples into one of the Duzzit's pipes.'

'*Lots* of gurples!' said Hannah. 'If we don't do something, they'll block the Duzzit and it will break!'

'Don't you worry, Hayseeds!' Olly

cried, leading all the others back to the machine.

'We'll protect you,' Hannah yelled over the Duzzit's noise, 'and we'll . . .' Her voice tailed away as the machine went, *Chug-a-chug-a cough cough chu-ug-uuuuh*. Then it was silent.

A gleeful 'Yibbeeee!' came from behind a tree. One Little Rotter

jumped into view, joyfully waving its

knobbly fists. 'We broked it. Lubbly,

lubbly, lubbly!' All the Little Rotters

ran off, shrieking with laughter.

Patch looked as if he was about to burst into tears. 'Oh my. *Now* what do we do?'

Purple Pie Attack

Everyone held their breath. Purple smoke belched out of the Duzzit's steam pipe. *Burrrrp!*

'It's burping!' Olly said, then he sniffed. 'What's that delicious smell?'

His mouth watered. It reminded him of . . .

'Hot chocolate cake!' Aidan cried, sniffing the air.

Olly shook his head, thinking. 'Nope . . . gingerbread.'

'Or maybe warm apple crumble?' suggested Hannah.

More purple smoke puffed out.

Burrrrp! Burrrrp!

Patch's face lit up. 'I think the Duzzit's going to be all right! It's not broken after all.'

A hatch in the Duzzit opened up, and a mechanical arm swung out. In its hand was . . . a freshly-baked pie! So that was what they could smell!

Another arm clanked out, holding

three dishes and three spoons. Then another with a little jug.

'Look!' said Hannah. 'The Duzzit's made us a pie with all that fruit. And there's cream too!'

'Let's try it.' Olly broke the pastry with his spoon and ate a mouthful. The fruit tasted sweeter than any he'd ever eaten – it was almost like

chocolate – and the pastry melted on his tongue.

Aidan and Hannah joined in. 'It's *gurple* pie!'

Patch smiled. 'I think that's the Duzzit's way of saying thank you for helping.'

'And we say a big thank you to the Duzzit!' said Aidan, who was on his second huge helping of pie.

'Mmmm, mmmmm! Yum!' Hannah mumbled through her purple-stained lips.

'I wish you Hayseeds could eat some pie,' said Olly.

'We do too,' said Sunny. But it goes straight through our straw.'

'None left anyway!' said Aidan,

scooping up the last pastry crumbs.

'It's fun watching you eat,' said Muck. 'You're as mucky as me!'

Hannah giggled, wiping her chin. 'Aidan. Cream. Nose!' she said.

Aidan stuck out his tongue and licked off the cream.

Clunk! The hatch opened and the Duzzit sent out a fresh pie.

Clunk! Another pie!

Clunk! Another!

Clunk! Clunk! Clunk!

'What are we going to do with all these?' asked Hannah. Olly shrugged, then . . .

'*Bobber, bobber, bobber*!'

'Little Rotters!' Olly hissed. 'Behind the mango tree.'

Four angry, gurple-stained faces
peered round one side of the tree
trunk. Three more faces appeared

round the other side. They muttered crossly.

'They're probably furious because their plan to break the Duzzit didn't work!' said Hannah.

Aidan's eyes twinkled. 'Pie?'

Olly nodded. 'Pie! Spread the word.'

While Aidan whistled as if nothing

interesting was happening, everyone grabbed a pie and held them ready – even the frightened Hayseeds.

'I never ever thought I'd be doing something like this,' murmured Muck.

'On three,' whispered Olly. 'One . . . two . . . *three!*'

Seven whole gurple pies whooshed

through the air, splatting into the mischievous Little Rotters' faces! Seven Little Rotters wobbled and then tumbled backwards.

Everyone cheered, but not for long! Once the Little Rotters had wiped pie out of their eyes, they scooped up all the messy fruit filling and started throwing it back.

Whoosh! A clump hit Olly on the chin. It felt disgusting as the sticky mush trickled down his neck. He wished they still had the umbrellas, but the Duzzit had tidied them away.

Whoosh! Aidan flung another pie.

The Hayseeds dived behind the Duzzit, but the children threw more mushy fruit and big chunks of pie.

The fruit fight carried on until the Little Rotters flopped down behind a tree. They peeped out, pointing and giggling.

Olly could see why. Everyone on the Duzzit was purple.

The Little Rotters ran off, still laughing. 'Filfy children! Filfy Duzzit! All filfy!'

Olly couldn't help smiling to himself. The Little Rotters were right – they were covered in fruit!

A Sweet Idea

Hannah stared at the sticky, splodgy Duzzit. 'What a mess.'

'Don't worry,' said Sunny. 'When something needs doing, the Duzzit does it!'

'That's right.' Muck licked a finger, pressed a button on the Duzzit and an arm appeared, holding a sponge that twinkled like snow.

Next, a green hose snaked out and squirted water all over the Duzzit. The sponge whizzed up and down, round and round, sending out silvery sparkles. Brightly coloured soapy bubbles floated around everywhere. In no time, the Duzzit gleamed.

Aidan grabbed the hose. 'Your turn for a wash, Olly!' he said, but the hose wriggled round and squirted Aidan instead! He squealed as the sparkling sponge scrubbed all traces of squashed fruit off him.

Hannah and Olly were laughing so

much they could hardly stand – until the hose turned on them! Brrr! It was cold, but fun, and everyone was splashed until they were spotless.

Olly asked the Hayseeds to join in, but Patch said that they couldn't. 'If we get too wet, we get soggy, and we have to spend all evening stuffing each other with fresh straw.'

Olly joined Hannah and Aidan, seeing who could slide furthest on the wet grass. Eventually, the hose flopped. No more water! The children started shivering.

'Come to the barn and dry off,' said Sunny. 'I'll show you how.' Off she ran.

'Race you,' Aidan said, challenging

Olly and Hannah. 'Last one there's a squashed gurple!'

In the barn, Sunny stood them on a circular plate on the floor. Instantly, a rail rose up around them. Olly wondered what was going to happen. You never knew on Magic Farm!

'Hold tight,' said Sunny. 'And . . . you're . . . *off*!'

The metal plate began to spin. Round they went, faster and faster, until Sunny was a blur.

'Whoooaaa!' cried Olly, as he found himself being pressed back against the rail. He squeezed his eyes tight shut. This was like a scary fairground ride.

'Aaaaaeeeeh!' squealed Hannah.

'It's . . . a . . . spin dryer!' yelled Aidan.

The metal plate finally slowed, and stopped. Olly noticed that Aidan's knuckles were white where he'd gripped the rail tightly. So he'd been scared too!

Hannah wobbled dizzily across the floor. 'Thanks, Sunny. We couldn't have explained our wet clothes to Mum and Dad!'

'Speaking of Mum and Dad,' said Olly, 'we'd better be going home.'

'You're right,' said Hannah, 'we should.'

As Patch took them to the spinning scarecrow, Olly said, 'I still don't understand why the gurples started growing and why the fruit here can just appear on *any* bush or tree.'

Patch smiled gently. 'On Magic Farm, some things are just . . . magic.'

Olly wasn't satisfied. He liked to know everything about the plants on Golden Valley Farm, and he felt the same about the ones here, too.

'I'll understand one day,' he told

the others. 'I'll even become a Magic Farm plant expert!' But now it was time to go.

Aidan held the scarecrow's arm first and ran round. Before he'd completed one full circle, he'd vanished. Next was Hannah. Then, with a cheery, 'Bye! We'll be back soon!' to Patch, Olly followed.

Magic Farm whooshed into a silvery blur and everything went silent until he bumped on to the Golden Valley hillside.

The three friends made their way back towards home. When they reached the farm, they saw the foal was stretching over the fence by Hannah's herb garden. Max sat close by, staring at her adoringly.

'Naughty foal!' scolded Hannah, but she couldn't help laughing. 'I'm growing those herbs to sell at the farmers' market! You shouldn't eat them!'

Olly stroked the foal's neck and tried, gently, to push her head away from the plants. 'Hey! That's strange,' he said. 'Her breath smells of mint.'

Aidan sniffed. 'Have you been eating minty sweeties?' he said. 'Naughty!'

'That's it!' said Olly. 'I know what we can call her.' He checked the label stuck in the ground beside the plant the foal had been nibbling. 'It's mint!' he said. 'These leaves are just like that plant the foal was eating earlier, so that must have been *wild* mint. That's one plant mystery solved. And a new name for her as well – Minty!'

'Minty the foal! I like it!' said Hannah.

Aidan picked a few leaves and sniffed them. 'That reminds me of . . . what? I know! Minty chocolate!'

Olly and Hannah stared at each other. Then, at the same time, they said, 'Oh *yes!*'

Aidan looked from one to the other.
'Huh?'

'Tomorrow we need to pick mint leaves,' said Hannah. 'If you help, we'll let you have a taste of our new ice-cream – *mint choc chip*!'

'Oooh, that sounds good!' said Aidan.

'The raspberry ripple must be

ready by now too,' added Hannah. 'Our ice-cream stand will be the star of the farmers' market!'

'If there's any left after Aidan gets to it!' Olly called as he followed the others.

The sun was setting as they trooped into the house for a taste of ice-cream.

'Wouldn't it be great if we could make gurple ice-cream!' said Aidan.

'It would,' agreed Olly. 'Nobody would be able to guess what the fruit was!'

'I love that Magic Farm is our own special secret,' said Hannah. 'I wonder what we'll discover next time we visit the Hayseeds?'

'Who knows!' replied Olly. 'There's always something exciting going on. Let's go back soon and find out!'

EGMONT PRESS: ETHICAL PUBLISHING

Egmont Press is about turning writers into successful authors and children into passionate readers – producing books that enrich and entertain. As a responsible children's publisher, we go even further, considering the world in which our consumers are growing up.

Safety First
Naturally, all of our books meet legal safety requirements. But we go further than this; every book with play value is tested to the highest standards – if it fails, it's back to the drawing-board.

Made Fairly
We are working to ensure that the workers involved in our supply chain – the people that make our books – are treated with fairness and respect.

Responsible Forestry
We are committed to ensuring all our papers come from environmentally and socially responsible forest sources.

For more information, please visit our website at
www.egmont.co.uk/ethicalpublishing

There's lots more fun to be had at **Magic Farm!**